CONTENTS

DeAth and the NEighBOurs At NesS

Old Nagger Barr keeps her farm next door to the graveyard at Ness. The lane past her door is the corpse path, where coffins bump by on the shoulders of men; it is the way to the grave for herself, and the neighbours.

4

One time, a long time ago, Nagger's young grandson arrived on the farm. His name was Fintan McGlone. Nagger was old even then, and Fintan had come to the farm in the hope he'd inherit when she died. Nagger Barr gave him his orders about how to do the different jobs on the farm, but he was lazy and he shirked the work. He made Nagger mad. She scolded and moaned and she chased him all day round the farm, though it didn't do her much good.

One day Nagger felt poorly, and so she called to the boy to come into the house.

"The way you go on, who's to care for the farm when I'm gone to the neighbours?" groaned old Nagger.

"What neighbours?" asked Fintan McGlone.

"The neighbours above that rest in their graves," said old Nagger. "I'm feared for the farm, once you get your hands on it, for you are no farmer."

"I'll do the job fine," Fintan said, thinking of how he would spend all the money that she'd kept hidden in jam jars all over her house.

6

"Well, mind that you do," scolded Nagger. "If you don't mend your ways and take care of my farm when I'm gone, I'll come back!"

Fintan grinned to himself. When you're dead, you stay dead. She couldn't come back, and she knew it, for all of her nagging. The nagging would stop when Nagger was brought to the grave...then Fintan would have his reward, for he'd have her good farm.

Soon after that old Nagger died, still groaning and moaning about whether Fintan would care for her farm, and keep things the way they should be.

Fintan had the wake for her that night along with his friends. Old Nagger was there, all dolled up in lace, set up in her coffin. It was laid out on a plank

and some chairs in the kitchen, after
the way at a wake.

"You'll never come back," Fintan
laughed down at old Nagger Barr in her
box. "You're dead and gone. From now
on, I'm having this farm," and he danced
around her with his friends.

Old Nagger Barr didn't stir. Death had her, and Death wasn't giving her back…or so Fintan thought.

Next day Fintan and his friends nailed the lid down and they carried old  Nagger along the corpse path to the graveyard at Ness. The priest said the prayers and they buried old Nagger way down in the earth. Then they went back to the house and they all ate and drank a bit more. After that, the others went back to their houses, and left Fintan alone, drinking and searching the place for old Nagger's jars full of money. He was up to all hours till he found them, with never a thought for the farm, or the beasts.

The night wore on, and Fintan went
to sleep by the fire in Nagger's old chair,
with a glass in his hand, and her jam jars
around him, all filled with her money,
well pleased now her money was his. He
went to sleep. He dreamed of how much
he would spend and how he would sell
up the farm, and open a
bar called The House
of McGlone, full of
hard drink that he'd
sell to his friends.
The best joke of it
was that her money
would pay for the
bar, which would
really have soured
poor old Nagger,
who never let drink
pass her lips.

Bang! came a knock at the door, and that woke Fintan up. It was a knock that would waken the dead, if Death let them wake, which Death wouldn't...or so Fintan thought.

"Who's that at this hour?" called Fintan McGlone from his seat by the fire.

"O'Riordan, your neighbour," a voice answered back from outside the door.

"The only O'Riordan I know was called Dan, and he died this yesteryear!" said Fintan McGlone.

"That's me," said the voice, greatly astonishing Fintan McGlone. He ran to the door and he pulled it wide open, thinking some of his friends had come to play a joke on him, after the death of old Nagger Barr.

Dan O'Riordan was there, large as life, but in death, for he wore his grave-clothes and he looked a bit gone, as well he might, having been dead for a year.

"Goodnight to you, Fintan," said O'Riordan. "I'm not coming in. I just called down to say that we're having trouble up there with old Nagger Barr. She's out of her box, and drifting around moaning about what you've been doing down here. She's nagging us all, and complaining, and we're getting no sleep in our graves."

"What ails the woman?" asked Fintan McGlone. "Isn't she dead? Why won't she lie down like her neighbours?"

"She's mad at you for not minding the cow," said O'Riordan. "It's out in the field and it's never been milked today, while you were in here drinking beer with your friends and counting her money. She says I'm to tell you, if you don't mend your ways, she'll come back to her farm."

"By jings, I forgot the old cow!"
said Fintan. "I'll deal with the cow,
and you can tell that to old Nagger,
like the good neighbour you are.
Tell her to mind she stays
put where she is with
the neighbours up
there in the grave,
for Death's put a
stop to her nagging
me, and this farm
is Fintan McGlone's.
It doesn't belong to
old Nagger Barr any
more, for she's dead."
    Fintan dealt with the cow,
and O'Riordan went back to
the graveyard above, but who
knows what he said to old Nagger,
or just how he put it.

That was all that
happened that night,
but the very next
night, as young
Fintan sat down to
his meal, there came
a *Bang! Bang!* at the door, so loud that
he choked on his food. He sprang up
from the table, and he almost broke the
fine china he'd bought for himself that
day at the shops, when he went down
to spend old Nagger's money.

"Who's that at my door?" called
Fintan McGlone.

"Your neighbour, Soraghan!"
answered a voice.

"Are you the Soraghan that's been
dead these long years?" said Fintan, for
he thought it might be, considering what
happened the evening before.

"That's right," said a voice. "Soraghan from out of the grave. I came down to say that your Nagger's making an awful fuss. She said to say you've not put the hens in, and you're spending her money on stuff that just isn't fit for a farmer. And we wouldn't mind that, but she's shouting at us, not at you, and we are too dead to look after your hens."

"The hens are all right where they are," said Fintan, opening the door to look at Soraghan, to check out that it was dead 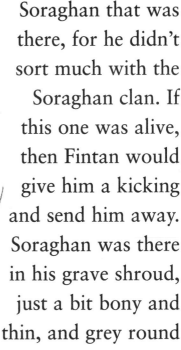Soraghan that was there, for he didn't sort much with the Soraghan clan. If this one was alive, then Fintan would give him a kicking and send him away. Soraghan was there in his grave shroud, just a bit bony and thin, and grey round the eyes. He'd gone quite a bit. Fintan could see the wall through him, so there was nothing worth kicking to kick.

18

"Now listen here, Fintan McGlone," said dead Soraghan. "You know and I know the hens are all right where they are, but old Nagger says that they're not, and she's scaring the neighbours above with her moaning and groaning. If you don't shape up, she swears she'll come back to her farm. Better put the hens in, and lay her to rest, or you'll have all of us down the lane haunting your house. Haunting you won't be easy for us, considering how long we've been dead, and Death doesn't like haunters one bit. But we'd do it just to be free of her nagging."

"I'm not scared of you graveyard people," said Fintan McGlone. "I can take care of an old pack of ghosts, and this farm is mine now. It has nothing to do with old Nagger."

"If you think so," said Soraghan, "it just goes to show that you don't know your Nagger."

The dead man was so cross he was grinding his teeth, which was a bit odd, considering how he had no teeth left to grind. The dead are like that. They do things for show when they're haunting.

The end of it
was Fintan got
the hens in, and
Soraghan went
back to his grave,
while Fintan was
counting the eggs.
The next night,
Fintan was watching
TV on a new set that he'd bought
with the egg-money.
There'd been a man
up from the town
to install it, and
now Fintan was
watching a horse
race, with the
form book
spread out
on his knee.

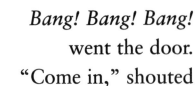

Bang! Bang! Bang!
went the door.
"Come in," shouted
Fintan McGlone, knowing
who it would be: some dead neighbour's
ghost come down from the graveyard
with more complaints from old Nagger
Barr and more of her threats that she'd
come back and haunt him.

"Are you asking me
in?" said a voice.
"Didn't I say so?" said
Fintan McGlone.
"Just wipe your
bones on the mat,
for that dust from
the grave is awful
messy, and I have had
my new carpet fitted and laid,
now I've got my hands on the money."

The door opened and in came a huge man all covered up in a black cloak and a hood, with a sack on his back. He laid the sack on Fintan's new blue carpet and he stood himself up by the fire. He was so big that he blocked the TV and Fintan missed the end of the race.

"Well, you're welcome here on my farm," said Fintan McGlone, running his mind down the list of the dead to think who this one might be, for he didn't look like one of the neighbours above in the graveyard, or not one that Fintan could recognise.

"It's not often I'm asked to come in," said the man.

Fintan thought a bit more, but he still couldn't put a name to the stranger before him. At last he said, "I'm ashamed to admit it, but though I'm sure I knew you well when you were alive, just now I can't put a name to your face."

"My name is Death," said the man, and he pulled down his hood and opened his cloak, so Fintan could see who he was.

All that Death had was dry bones, and no flesh at all, no eyes, no nose, no nails on his fingers and toes, though he'd rotting black teeth that he showed as he grinned at Fintan and spoke. "I called in to leave you this sack."

"What's in the sack?" asked Fintan McGlone, a little bit alarmed to think he was talking to Death. Death belonged with the neighbours who slept in the graveyard next door, and didn't belong in the house.

"I've brought Nagger back," said Death, and he tumbled the old woman out on the floor from the sack. "She doesn't like your ways so she's scolding and moaning and groaning about, and spoiling the peace of the grave for the others, and all on account of your wrecking her farm, and spending her money like water. It's all your fault. That's why you're getting her back, because the neighbours up there can't abide her." Then Death twirled his cloak and swirled up the chimney and vanished.

Fintan looked down at old Nagger, who still seemed very dead as she lay on the new carpet he'd put on the floor. Then she stirred a bit, and her eyes opened wide, and she grinned up at Fintan, delighted.

"I said I'd come back to my farm," she told Fintan. "I'm back, alive, and I'm staying, and bad cess to you, young McGlone!"

They're both there to this day on the farm, on the corpse path to the graveyard at Ness. Old Nagger Barr won't leave her farm till Fintan McGlone has mended his ways, and Fintan's still hoping she'll drop down and leave him her money one day and so... Fintan's waiting for Death to come to the door, but Death won't be calling for Nagger just yet...

Death's not letting her back in the graveyard at Ness, he's not letting her back, for she was upsetting the neighbours, poor souls.

Little Bridget

Bridget O'Flynn was a wild little child who liked playing about in the field.

"Don't be alone in the field or the fairies will get you!" her mother told her. But Bridget had no fear of the fairies, for they'd never caught her before, though she often played in the field when her brothers and sisters were out.

One day Bridget stayed in the field far too long, and dusk came, and Bridget was cold coming home and her legs had an ache from her running about, and she caught a stone in her shoe.

She sat down and took her shoe off, and shook out the stone.

Then she heard a small sound, like the music that's made by a river, although there was no river there.

She sat still and listened, and somehow the soft music sent her to sleep.

Maybe she dreamt that she heard
a strange singing and dancing and
laughing and larking about, and maybe
she went to see what it was
that was making such
a noise in her field.
Maybe she did and
maybe she didn't.
It may be that
she wasn't
dreaming at all,
but awake in
her sleep and
bewitched. Maybe
she saw some Little
Things in the corn,
and some more Little
Things dancing and prancing
around. Maybe some of
the Little Things called her by name.

31

"Bridget O'Flynn! You're wanted below!"

"Bridget O'Flynn! Follow us in!"

"Bridget O'Flynn! You'll not have us waiting for you!"

Maybe she followed them down the field to a hole in the ground that she'd not seen before, there by the thorn tree. Maybe there was no hole in the ground. Maybe it never was there.

Maybe she went in.

She never came home to her father and mother, Phelim and Mary O'Flynn.

The family searched high and low, high and low, Phelim and Mary O'Flynn, and her sisters and brothers, Anna and Seamus, Maureen and Joe, John Paul and Patrick. All of the neighbours came out and helped in the search for the little O'Flynn that was lost in the field: McCann the milkman, and the family O'Boyle who had the top field, and the Meehans from over the brae, and McGraw from Glenowen. They all were out looking for Bridget O'Flynn, that maybe the fairies had stolen away.

All they found was one yellow shoe that Bridget had left where she stopped to take out the stone that was bothering her foot. She left the yellow shoe there on the ground, never knowing she'd left it behind her.

They thought Little Bridget was dead and they grieved after her. They kept her place by the fire for a long time, just in case she'd come home, but she didn't.

Little Bridget was gone and almost forgotten, though they had a Mass said each year on her saint's day.

The years passed away and so did her father and mother, Phelim and Mary O'Flynn. They are buried below in Ramore. Her sisters and brothers died too, one by one. Seamus passed on with the fever and Maureen was too good to live, so she died, when she wasn't much older than Bridget. Joe lived to be old, but he died as well, and John Paul and Patrick were lost in the war.

Bridget's whole family were dead, except for Anna, who wed and had sons and a daughter who all but one upped and left her and went to the States. One stayed on the farm. That was young Phelim. One son was all the small farm could keep.

After her husband had died and passed on, Anna worked on the farm with young Phelim. They did very well, for they worked very hard to look after the land that looked after them. They sold their crops and their cattle, and they bought up more land in the years that were good.

Fourscore years
and more passed
Anna by, till she grew
old and weak and sat
by the fire with her
stick, for she couldn't
work any more. Her son, the young
Phelim, aged fifty, was running the farm,
and a fine farm it was, for he had the
land that belonged to the O'Boyles,
and the land of the Meehans, and the
bog lake forbye that used to belong to
McGraw. The old neighbours were gone
to the grave, and their children had
moved to the city for work.

Only Anna was left from the old times,
biding her time by the fire, and she
hadn't the strength in her legs to go out
of the house, or the power in her eyes
to see to the tip of her nose.

It was late one night, and Anna sat crouched by the fire, a slave to rheumatism and gout. There was a knock at the door, but Anna was too old to answer, and Phelim was over the way helping out at the house of the priest, Father O'Rawe.

The door opened wide, and in came a small child with one shoe on its foot, the other foot bare.

The child came up to Anna, face on, and she said: "Who are you? Why are you here in our house?" just like that.

Now Anna, half blind, couldn't see much of the child, just a blur, but she prodded the child with the tip of her stick, in case it would step on her foot that was sore with the gout.

"Why are you here in our house?" asked the child, sounding scared.

"Whose house do you think you're in?" answered Anna, quite sharp, although something stirred in her that bothered her mind. Maybe it was the voice of the child, for somehow she thought she knew it.

"Our house, O'Flynn's!" cried the child. "Where is my mammy?"

"Your mammy?" said Anna. "There's no mammy here!"

"And where is my daddy and sisters and brothers?" the child said, with tears in her voice.

"Hush, child, don't cry," said Anna.

The child wouldn't be hushed.

She turned right around, looking at all the new things in the room.

"Where's our mammy's chair and the clock on the wall, and who is that man coming in by our door?"

It was Phelim who'd come in through the door. He looked at the strange child, with one shoe, and he didn't know her from Eve.

He thought she was a gypsy come from the field, to rob or to steal from his mother.

"Have you no home to go to? Get out of this house!" said Phelim. "And don't you be teasing my old wheezy mother!"

The child fled from the house.

"Are you right now, Mammy?" Phelim said to his mother.

"The right leg is terrible sore," answered Anna, clutching her stick, for she was feeling the pain from the gout.

"Who was that child?" asked Phelim.

"I don't know at all," Anna said. "But she had the sound of our Bridget."

"Bridget?" said Phelim.

"The little one that the fairies stole from the field long ago, before you were thought of," said Anna.

"I doubt that," said Phelim. "She'd be an old woman like you if she'd lived, not a young child with one shoe."

And that was the end of their talk.

It wasn't the end of the child with
one shoe.

The child with one shoe lay out
in the corn.

She'd only been asleep in that field
for a minute, it seemed, and she thought
that she'd dreamt something strange,
and then she woke up and found
that she'd lost her shoe, and she
thought she'd be scolded by Mammy.

But there was no Mammy there in the house, and no Daddy, no sister or brother or kin, just an old woman who sat by the fire and a man who came in that she'd not seen before, in a house that was all changed and different, though it seemed to be the house that she knew.

She lay and she sobbed till the Little Things came and found their friend out in the corn. They brought her back to the hole in the field near the thorn trees and they welcomed her in.

Bridget O'Flynn is playing there still with her friends, underground.

She thinks she's been there for an hour, maybe a little bit more. But an hour down below in their hole in the ground is many a year for Bridget O'Flynn, the girl with the stone in her shoe who slept in the corn. Her lifetime is gone.

Now no one remembers her name.

More about the Stories...

These stories are all my own work, but they are meant to sound and feel like the stories told by a Seancaiti, the gaelic word for a storyteller.

Imagine the loneliness of a tiny cottage on a bog road, the pitch darkness outside, the firelight and the smells of the turf. There were hidden meanings in the old stories, for those who had learned how to listen!

Martin Waddell

SOFT BUTTER'S GHOST

Laughing at fear...

"Doing a deal with death" stories are common the world over, and this one is a bad case of graveyard disturbance, leading to a ghostly version of a knock-knock joke, with unfresh corpses calling at Old Nagger's farm to complain about her grandson, Fintan McGlone.

Some people fear dying, and try to cope with their fear by telling stories that laugh at it. This is what this story does.

Personally, I liked the idea of poor old Death having problems with one of the dead who just wouldn't lie down.

LITTLE BRIDGET

...or trying to explain it away.

As well as death, many people fear the unknown. Instead of laughing at it, they might try to cope with their fear by telling stories that offer explanations of the inexplicable.

There is an Irish poem by William Allingham called "The Fairies". One line of it reads: "When she came back, her friends were all gone." That was my starting point in writing this story. Worldwide, there are versions of the human-taken-by-the fairies tales which deal with the question of someone disappearing without trace. *Rip Van Winkle* is a well-known American example of such a tale. Most of these stories have the fairies living underground, and this probably has something to do with the existence of ancient burial mounds. In Ireland there are also underground chambers known as souterrains. It is not absolutely certain what they were used for in ancient times, but people knew they were there, hidden under the fields, and legends grew up round them.

The not-very-hidden message in this story is: *Don't be wandering off with strangers, or you never know what may happen!*

Tales of Ghostly Ghouls and Haunting Horrors!

"Every story creates that sense of uneasiness which is experienced when a door creaks or a window rattles." *Carousel*

Written by Martin Waddell
Illustrated by James Mayhew

SOFT BUTTER'S GHOST
and Himself   *ISBN 1 84362 430 3*

BONELESS AND THE TINKER
and Dancing with Francie   *ISBN 1 84362 431 1*

GALLOWS HILL
and The Ghostly Penny   *ISBN 1 84362 432 X*

DEATH AND THE NEIGHBOURS AT NESS
and Little Bridget   *ISBN 1 84362 433 8*

All at £3.99

Orchard Myths are available from all good bookshops,
or can be ordered direct from the publisher:
Orchard Books, PO BOX 29, Douglas IM99 1BQ
Credit card orders please telephone 01624 836000
or fax 01624 837033
or e-mail: bookshop@enterprise.net for details.

To order please quote title, author and ISBN
and your full name and address.
Cheques and postal orders should be
made payable to 'Bookpost plc'.
Postage and packing is FREE within the UK
(overseas customers should add £1.00 per book).

Prices and availability are subject to change.